D1592114

the Night Owl

by Kim C. Lee

ISBN: 978-0-578-71269-7 (paperback)

Printed in the United States of America

~ Dedication ~

For Jourden, who has inspired me to reach farther
than I ever planned and kept me up at night
so that I could do so.

~ Acknowledgments ~

I wish to thank Aaliyah Hill for contributing her time and
beautiful artwork. I would also like to thank Lynda Mallory
who provided valuable guidance and insight on my journey
to bring this story to life.

"Time's up! Its 8:00pm! Make your way upstairs!"

In the midst of playing,
this is the worst thing to hear!

I prefer to stay up, instead of laying down.
The idea of snoozing leaves me with a frown.
At night after bedtime is when the action happens!
This is when you will find all the fun that's worth having!

Once the lights go out and the room is filled with darkness, I'm free to slide out of bed or jump on my mattress.

I love counting the stars
and making new friends.
I dance with the shadows
and sing, sing, sing!

I turn on my flashlight to check for monsters.
Are they under the bed or hiding in closets?

Are there creepy creatures trying to get free?
No, just some familiar faces looking at me!

I wonder if Mommy knows I'm not asleep.
I tiptoe to her room to take a little peek.

"I see you my little night owl, and I love you dear."

"Back into your room and back into your bed."
She takes me by the hand and to my room I am led.

"Do I have to go to bed? I'd rather stay awake."

"*Even night owls at some point need to take a break.*"

I settle into my pillow to get real "comfy".
After all that fun, my eyes start to get heavy.
I fight to stay awake just a little bit longer,
But slumber is calling and too strong to conquer.

Before I know it, I'm sound asleep.
No more ruffling in the darkness, not even a peep.

CPSIA information can be obtained
at www.ICGtesting.com
Printed in the USA
LVHW071651220121
677209LV00018B/2877